LITTLE JACK HORNER

LIVE

FROM THE CORNER

Helaine Becker

illustrations by

Mike Boldt

Scholastic Canada Ltd.
Toronto New York London Auckland Sydney
Mexico City New Delhi Hong Kong Buenos Aires

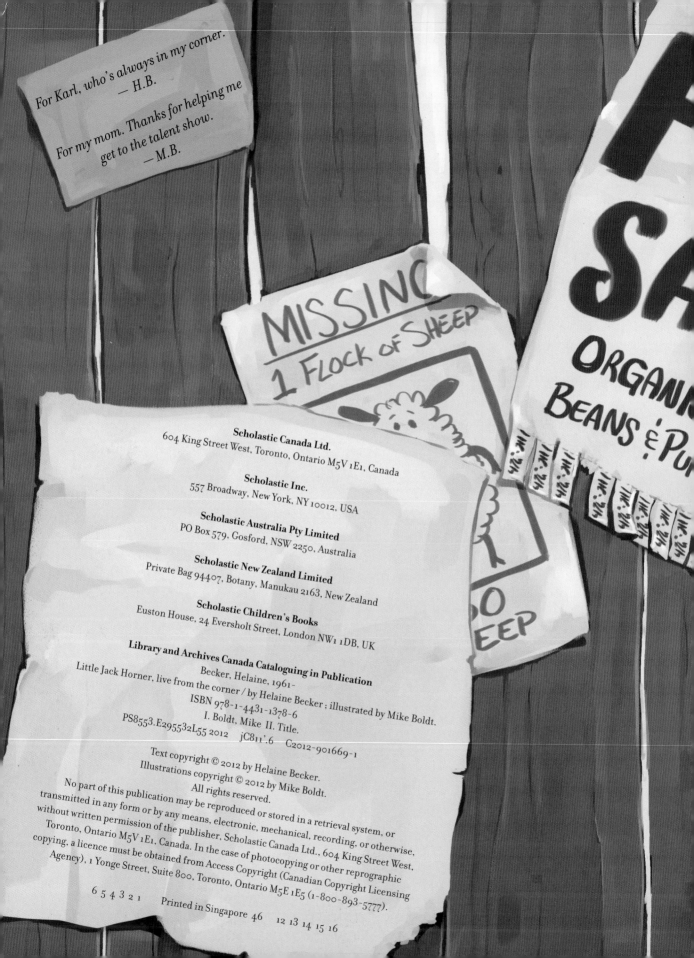

For Karl, who's always in my corner.
— H.B.

For my mom. Thanks for helping me
get to the talent show.
— M.B.

MISSING
1 Flock of Sheep

Scholastic Canada Ltd.
604 King Street West, Toronto, Ontario M5V 1E1, Canada

Scholastic Inc.
557 Broadway, New York, NY 10012, USA

Scholastic Australia Pty Limited
PO Box 579, Gosford, NSW 2250, Australia

Scholastic New Zealand Limited
Private Bag 94407, Botany, Manukau 2163, New Zealand

Scholastic Children's Books
Euston House, 24 Eversholt Street, London NW1 1DB, UK

Library and Archives Canada Cataloguing in Publication
Becker, Helaine, 1961-
Little Jack Horner, live from the corner / by Helaine Becker ; illustrated by Mike Boldt.
ISBN 978-1-4431-1378-6
I. Boldt, Mike II. Title.
PS8553.E295532L55 2012   jC811'.6   C2012-901669-1

6 5 4 3 2 1   Printed in Singapore 46   12 13 14 15 16

Ma Goose Farms
Presents
So You Think
You Can
Rhyme?
Come out to TALENT TIME
Singers, Dancers, Pipers, Bakers and Candlestick Makers
- All are Welcome -
Present Your Unique Vocal Stylings
for a Chance to WIN A GOLDEN GOOSE!
Hosted by M.C.:
Humpty "I am the Eggman" Dumpty

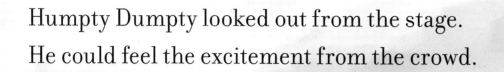

Humpty Dumpty looked out from the stage. He could feel the excitement from the crowd.

"How's everybody doing?" shouted Humpty, egging the crowd on. "You all know our first performer. It took some coaxing but he's decided to come out of the corner. So let's give him a great big hand. Let's hear it for . . .

LITTLE JACK HORNER!"

Little Jack Horner cleared his throat. "Er . . . okay. Hi. I've got a little song for you folks today. It's an old favourite of mine, and probably one of yours, too."

Then Jack began to sing:

"Old MacDonald had a farm
and Bingo was his name-o . . ."

Suddenly a voice called out,
"Excuse me, Mr. Horner,
but that's not right!"

Mary, Mary, Quite Contrary had jumped to her feet.

"The farmer's name isn't Bingo, sir," said Mary, Mary. "His name is Fred. Fred MacDonald. His *dog's* name is Bingo."

Jack squinted out at the audience.

"Really? So sorry. My mistake."

He retuned his banjo and continued his song:

"Ahem . . . *And on that farm he had some sheep—*"

But Mary, Mary, Quite Contrary was right back up
on her feet.

"Excuse me, but that's not right," she huffed.
"That Little Bo Peep . . . she's such a scatterbrain!
She lost her sheep and doesn't know where to find them.
There are no sheep on Old MacDonald's farm. Not one."

Little Jack Horner blushed. "Really? So sorry. My mistake. Again," he said.

Not even daring to look in Mary, Mary's direction, he started up his song once more:

"And on that farm he had some goats—"

Mary, Mary, Quite Contrary was flapping her arms in the air.

"What is it now?" demanded Little Jack Horner, wishing he'd just stayed home in his nice comfy corner.

"That's not right either," Mary, Mary declared.
"The three billy goats went trippety-trop, trippety-trop, trippety-trop, over the bridge to the meadow.
They had a bit of a bother getting there, too, with the troll trying to eat them and all."

"Is that so?" Jack replied. "I hadn't heard. So sorry.

Little Jack Horner cleared his throat nervously, then launched back into his song:

"And on that farm he had some cows—"

This time Jack stopped himself.
"Wait. Don't tell me. No cows either, right?"

"Jumped over the moon. Not seen since,"
replied Mary, Mary.

"Any geese?"

"No," said Mary, Mary. "Goosey Loosey went with Chicken Little to tell the Queen the sky was falling. That was the last we saw of good ol' Loosey. Miss Little, too.

"Pigs?" Jack asked.

"Oh, those three moved out," said Mary, Mary. "They built a few houses and had some trouble with a wolf. But they're doing swell now. They're living together in that little brick home."

Now, Little Jack Horner was a good boy but even he'd had enough of Mary, Mary's contrariness. "That's all interesting," he said. "But I'm trying to sing a song here."

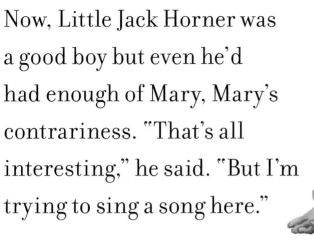

"Sorry," said Mary, Mary quite contritely. "I'll just sit with my silver bells and cockleshells, and pretty maids all in a row."

"Not. So. Fast," said Jack. "Before I start singing, tell me EVERYTHING I need to know about that farm. Any cats on it?"

"No. That Puss found some boots and set off to find his fortune."

"Ducks?"

"One, but she turned into a swan then headed off to Hollywood," replied Mary, Mary.

"Mice?" Jack squeaked. "There *must* be mice!"

Mary, Mary sighed. "At first we thought Mick had just run up the town clock and he'd be right back. But then the clock got stuck at 12:59 and he still hasn't run back down."

Jack threw his hands in the air. "So why don't you just tell me already? What animals are on that old farm?"

Mary, Mary shouted right back: "I already told you . . ."

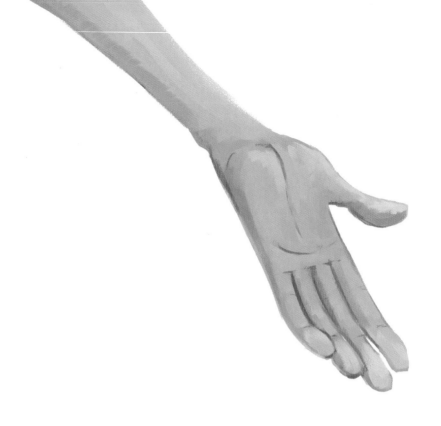

"...there's the DOG!"

"BINGO is his name-o!"

Jack grinned at the crowd.
"All together now:

B-I-N-G-O

B-I-N-G-O

B-I-N-G-O

And Bingo is his name-o!"